Fearsome Four

The Ghost of the Rickety House

Joseph Jethro

ISBN: 978-1-917452-21-2

josephjethro45@outlook.com

More Titles By Joseph Jethro:

- Fearsome Four: The Zombies of the Moonlit Marshes

Contents

Chapter One

'He hit me first!' Umari yelled, jabbing a finger at Ray and spitting in his face.

'No, *you* hit me first!' Ray shot back, his glare sharper than a porcupine's quills.

Abner, their older brother, stood a few steps away, arms folded like a strict teacher. He watched the two quarrel. Shaking his head with an air of exaggerated authority, he announced in his most serious voice, 'You both need a timeout.'

Ray and Umari paused, their eyes locking in a sharp, disapproving stare.

'*Excuse me*!' Ray's tone was sharp as he jabbed an accusing finger at Umari. 'Why do *I* need a timeout when *he's* the one who started it?'

'Don't act like an idiot, Abner. You're not my mum that you're telling me to stand in timeout!' Umari chimed in, crossing his arms defiantly.

'Don't call me an idiot!' Abner snapped back; his tone didn't sound like a 'wise teacher' anymore; instead, he sounded like an 'angry kid'. 'I'm your big brother, and you must listen to me!'

The argument escalated rapidly into a full-blown shouting match, their voices echoing through the trees and startling nearby birds into flight.

Meanwhile, Sani, the second eldest brother, was busy chasing a squirrel through the meadow. But when he heard the yelling, he couldn't resist investigating. He trotted over just in time to see the chaos escalate.

As Umari gave Abner a hefty shove, Abner's green glasses flew off his face like a startled grasshopper.

The glasses sailed through the air, flipping once, twice - then straight over Sani's head.

'Really?' Sani huffed. 'Are you guys fighting again?' He rolled his eyes and bent down to pick up Abner's glasses, but as his fingers reached for them, he froze mid-motion. The glasses were no longer there.

'Wait...what?' Sani whispered, twisting his head sharply. He turned and scanned the area, but the glasses were nowhere to be found.

'Guys!' he called out, but his brothers were still too busy arguing to notice. 'GUYS!' Sani roared, his voice cutting through their bickering like a thunderclap.

All three brothers stopped mid-argument and turned towards him, blinking like startled owls.

'Where are my glasses?' Abner asked, squinting at the ground.

'That's what I'm trying to tell you!' Sani groaned. 'They were right here a second ago, and now they're gone!'

'There they are!' Umari suddenly shouted, bouncing on his toes and pointing excitedly towards something in the distance.

'Oh no!' Abner moaned, following Umari's gaze. 'That squirrel's got my glasses! GET HIM!'

With a war cry that would've made a knight proud, Abner charged after the squirrel.

'I don't think that was such a great idea,' Ray said, grinning as the squirrel darted off with the glasses clamped in its tiny mouth. It bolted across the meadow, with Abner hot on its heels, and disappeared into a cluster of massive trees that stretched high into the sky.

Sani rolled his eyes, clearly unimpressed, and gestured for the others to follow as he sprinted after Abner.

'The guy's completely nuts,' Ray said with a smirk, trailing behind Sani. 'Who chases a squirrel? It's not like the little furball will stop and hand over the glasses.'

'I never knew squirrels liked glasses,' Umari said, raising an eyebrow.

'I mean, seriously, right? It's bizarre!' Sani laughed, keeping pace with Abner, who had already barrelled into the dense trees.

'Oh, no!' Ray muttered, squeezing his eyes shut. 'Abner's gonna run straight into a tree!'

Abner suddenly shrieked as he ran straight into a tree trunk with a loud, cartoonish thud, crumpling to the ground in a dazed heap.

'Are you okay?' Sani panted, kneeling beside him.

'Yeah,' Abner chuckled weakly, his cheeks red with embarrassment and frustration. 'If I had my glasses, I don't think I would've run into that stupid tree,' he grumbled, slowly pulling himself up.

Ray couldn't contain his grin. 'Shame on you!' he sneered.

Sani gave Ray a firm smack on the back of the head. 'Cut it out, Ray,' he said, his tone serious. 'We must find that dumb squirrel and get his glasses back.' He gazed at the towering trees, scanning for the elusive rodent.

'This is the eleventh pair of glasses you've lost. Mum's not gonna be happy about this,' Umari sighed.

'It's your fault for pushing me,' Abner muttered, walking behind Sani.

'Hey, there it is!' Umari yelled, pointing at a tree. The group looked up to see the squirrel perched on a branch, wearing

Abner's glasses like a cool dude and casually flicking a peanut into its mouth.

'Is it just me, or does that creepy rodent look like it's smirking at us?' Umari said, raising an eyebrow.

'Is it just me, or does it look like your eyebrows are about to fly off?' Ray shot back, smirking.

Sani grinned. 'Yeah, seriously, bro. Quit raising them like that. They're almost touching the clouds.'

The group shifted their attention to the squirrel, which flicked a peanut straight at Abner, hitting him square on the nose. 'Ouch, my nose!' he yelped, hopping around and rubbing his face.

The squirrel, unbothered, started lobbing peanuts at them. They jumped and dodged, frantically trying to avoid the shower of snacks flying at them.

Suddenly, a hissing whisper slithered through the air, chilling them to the bone. All four of them froze, their breath catching in their throats. The squirrel squealed in fright and darted into a hole in the tree trunk, dropping Abner's glasses, which clattered to the ground with an eerie echo.

'W-what w-was that?' Umari stammered, his voice trembling as he hid behind Sani.

'It was nothing,' Abner muttered, bending down to grab his glasses. He quickly put them on and scowled at Umari. 'It was just the wind or your smelly fart. Now, let's get back to the meadow before Dad starts asking Mum where in the world we have gone.'

'Y-yeah, let's g-get out of here!' Umari's voice trembled.

'Stop it, Umari,' Abner said firmly, his tone growing more assertive. 'It was just the wind.'

But before anyone could move, cold, twisted laughter slithered through the air, sending an icy shiver down their spines. The sound was so unnatural and horrifying that it froze them in their tracks.

Chapter Two

'Remember that morning when something – or someone – knocked on our bedroom window?' Abner said, his voice low as his eyes darted around.

'Yeah, I do,' Ray replied, his gaze sweeping nervously over the trees and bushes.

'It had to be a ghost knocking on our window,' Abner whispered, sinking into the tall grass. 'And I think that same ghost is right here. Watching and listening.'

The other three brothers sank into the grass beside him, sweat dripping down their backs.

'A g-g-ghost?' Umari stammered, his face pale. 'Ghosts aren't real, Abner. S-stop trying to scare me,' he said, biting his bottom lip, though his shaking voice betrayed his fear.

'Guys...look,' Ray hissed, pointing towards the cobbled path.

A faint white glow hovered just above the path, flickering like a candle in the wind.

All four gasped as the glow grew brighter, its edges shimmering unnaturally.

Raindrops began to fall, pattering against the ground. Then, with a sudden, blinding crack, lightning split the sky. Angry grey clouds swallowed the once bright and sunny day. Thunder boomed, shaking the ground beneath them, and Umari shrieked, nearly falling over in fright.

The eerie white glow twisted and shifted until it formed the outline of a figure. Ray's breath hitched as he gasped, 'Oh...what in the world of monsters is *that*?'

The pale, glowing figure snapped its head sharply in their direction. Flattening themselves into the grass, they sought better concealment, their hearts pounding furiously. Abner pressed a trembling finger to his lips, signalling them to stay silent.

The figure was ghostly white, draped in what appeared to be a flowing robe that shimmered like mist. Its long, ethereal hair, which reached far past its hips, drifted unnaturally as though caught in an invisible breeze. But its eyes were the most horrifying of all. They glowed a piercing, blood-red hue, filled with a hunger that made their skin crawl as if it were searching for prey.

It began to float towards them, the faint sound of its movements like whispers in the air. The four brothers held their breaths, their bodies trembling as the creature drew closer.

The figure stopped, its glowing eyes cutting through the dense, shadowy grass. It appeared to gaze directly into the spot where they were hiding, leaving them frozen in tense silence.

Then, with an eerie twist of its head, it turned and floated up the cobbled path, its ghostly form disappearing.

As the figure vanished up the path, Abner let out a shaky whisper. 'That was a close one... like, what the heck was that creature?' he muttered, wiping raindrops off his lenses.

'It looked like a ghost to me,' Sani said, glancing uneasily at the empty path.

'A f-freaky one,' Umari stuttered, hugging himself as the drizzle turned heavier. 'And I'm not in the mood for rain! I'm in summer clothes, not winter gear,' he groaned, shivering as the dampness clung to him.

'Let's head back to Mum and Dad. They'll be waiting for us,' Sani sighed, standing up and brushing wet grass off his knees.

'Are you crazy?' Abner hissed, grabbing Sani's hand to stop him. 'Let's follow that ghost!' His grin was a mix of excitement and defiance.

'Are you *bonkers*?' Umari snapped, his voice rising in panic. 'That thing looked like it wanted to suck on someone's blood!'

'But…there's no harm in just seeing where it went,' Abner said, his eyes sparkling mischievously despite the eerie atmosphere. He flashed a cheeky smile. 'Come on, we'll just walk a little up the path and see if it's still there.'

'Hmmm, I'm not sure this is a good idea. Besides, ghosts can't be real,' Sani said, folding his arms sternly.

'But that's what you said about zombies,' Ray said, glancing around nervously as though expecting a monster to leap out at any moment.

'Fine,' Sani huffed. 'We're the Fearsome Four – what do we have to worry about?'

'Yeah!' Ray shouted, his voice full of excitement as he raised his fist in the air.

'Fearsome Four!' they all yelled, giving each other a high-five with grins that didn't quite mask their nerves.

They scrambled out of the long grass and cautiously approached the cobbled path.

'I wish I had a raincoat,' Abner groaned, his teeth clattering. 'Isn't it weird how the weather just suddenly changed?'

'It might have something to do with that ghost,' Umari said, his voice low and uneasy.

'That doesn't sound good,' Sani muttered, taking the lead as they began walking up the cobbled path.

The rain fell steadily, forming shallow puddles that splashed beneath their feet.

Their shoes squelched with each cautious step. Eyes darting nervously, they glanced at the shadows around them, every rustling leaf and snapping twig making their hearts race faster.

After what felt like an eternity, Abner came to a sudden halt. 'Oh boy, oh boy,' he stated, his mouth hanging open like a goldfish, eyes wide with disbelief. 'What in the world *is* this?' he gasped, staring at the enormous house looming before them.

They had never seen a house like this before – it was strange, captivating, and utterly unfamiliar. It stood tall and imposing, its crooked silhouette casting eerie shadows in the dim light of the stormy evening. The walls were a patchwork of weathered stone and dark, rotting wood, sagging and creaking as though the house was groaning under the weight of its age. The jagged and uneven roof appeared as if it might collapse with every gust of wind. Ivy twisted up the walls like tendrils of some ancient, forgotten creature, its leaves blackened and withered.

But what caught their attention the most was the upstairs window. A flickering candlelight danced in the gloom behind the glass, casting an eerie glow onto the peeling shutters.

Abner swallowed hard, his voice barely a whisper. 'What do you think is in there?'

Chapter Three

'Let's head back to the meadow,' Umari suggested, pausing briefly before turning and walking confidently down the cobbled path.

Sani shot a nervous glance at Abner before cautiously inching towards the house's front door. His fingers wrapped around the icy doorknob, turning it with deliberate care, but the door refused to budge.

'It's locked,' Sani whispered, glancing over his shoulder at Ray and Abner.

'Oh, that's just great,' Abner groaned, shaking his head. His eyes scanned the house, his frown reflecting a growing sense of unease. Then he headed towards the back. Ray and Sani followed quickly, rain drenching their dark hair.

'I knew it,' Abner said, a smug grin spreading across his face as they reached the backside. He pointed triumphantly at a gaping hole in the wall, where bricks were missing.

'What do you think you're doing?' Umari's sudden, sharp voice made them all jump. They turned to see him sneaking up behind them and instinctively clutched their chests, startled.

'You scared the crap out of me,' Ray gasped, his heart still racing.

'Are you guys out of your minds? This place is cursed! Why would you even think about going inside? Are you trying to become ghost busters?' Umari snapped, his voice rising as he placed his hands on his hips, glaring at them.

'If you're feeling too scared, you can stay here instead of going inside,' Sani said, eyeing the dark, gaping hole in the wall. 'We're just gonna take a quick look inside this old wreck.' He stepped forward and jumped through the hole, disappearing into the shadows.

'Fine, I'll stay out here. I'm not stupid like you guys,' Umari spat, saliva spraying onto Ray's cheek.

'Are you kidding me?!' Ray shouted, grimacing as he swiped at the spit on his cheek. Without further hesitation, he followed Abner into the pitch-black void, leaving Umari transfixed, caught in the grip of fear, his heart pounding.

'You guys are insane! You're not leaving me out here alone!' Umari shouted after them, his voice trembling. He looked around, his breath coming in quick, shallow gasps.

Then suddenly, a soft voice drifted through the cold air. 'I don't think you want to stay out here, little one...'

Umari froze, a shiver running down his spine. He spun around to see where the voice had come from but saw no one. 'Aaaaaaagh!' he screamed, his voice high-pitched with terror.

He quickly jumped straight into the hole and dashed after the others, sweat trickling down his forehead.

'So, you really wanted to come, huh?' Ray mocked, raising an eyebrow.

'Something's following us...we need to get out of here,' Umari said, his body trembling.

'Scaredy cat,' Abner teased, sticking out his tongue and wiggling his butt like a silly caterpillar.

They crept down a long, dark hallway. A faded red rug stretched across the floor, and eerie portraits of people lined the walls, making the house feel haunted.

'It feels like those people in the pictures are staring at us,' Umari muttered, his voice shaky. 'Maybe they're trying to warn us to get out of this sinister house,' he added, quickly turning a corner.

'Very funny...' Ray said, his voice trailing off. 'Wait, what's that noise? And why is the ground shaking?' His heart raced as he gulped nervously.

In stunned silence, they turned to see a chaotic scene unfold – a herd of wild white horses charging down the hallway, their hooves thundering against the ground, sending tremors through the walls. The ceiling quaked, and the chandeliers swung wildly as frames and artwork crashed to the floor in a rain of shattered glass.

'AAAHH!' the four brothers screamed, tumbling over each other as they scrambled to outrun the galloping horses.

But they were no match for the speed of the herd. The horses closed in, racing straight towards them. With no time to escape, the four of them dropped to the floor, bracing for impact, their arms around each other, eyes squeezed shut in fear.

'I don't want to DIE!' shrieked Umari.

The deafening sound of thundering hooves grew louder, and they tensed, preparing themselves for the inevitable impact. But instead of the anticipated crushing blow, there was nothing. The sound continued to grow, growing ever more intense, yet there was no trace of pain.

Ray slowly opened one eye, then released a sharp gasp of shock, and the others quickly followed suit, their expressions frozen in disbelief. The horses were charging straight over them, but their hooves were like wisps of smoke, passing through the air without touching them.

'This is amazing!' Abner gulped, his eyes wide as he watched the massive horses gallop over them, their hooves fading into the distance, leaving only an eerie, heavy silence in their wake.

'That was insane!' Ray grinned, shaking with adrenaline as he stood up.

'Hey, my glasses!' Abner suddenly shouted.

The brothers turned just in time to see Abner sprinting down the hallway. His eyes locked onto his glasses, floating eerily in the air, just out of his reach.

'H-His g-glasses…a-are they FLOATING?!' Umari's voice broke, filled with terror. His panicked cry sent Ray and Sani stumbling back, their faces pale and stricken as the unthinkable scene finally registered.

Chapter Four

'Abner! Abner!' Ray shouted. 'Where are you?' He looked back at Sani and Umari, who were nervously scanning the dark corners of a room they had walked into. Abner had disappeared while chasing his floating glasses, and now they were left in this crumbling, abandoned house with no sign of him.

'ABNER!' Umari yelled, frustration rising in his voice. 'This is *your* fault we're stuck in this creepy house! And now you've gone and vanished!'

A blood-curdling scream shattered the silence, sending a cold shiver down their spines. The hair on their necks stood up as the noise reverberated off the walls.

'That was Abner, wasn't it?' Ray whispered, his face as pale as the moon. His eyes filled with fear, a tear slipping down his cheek.

'Do you think he was...trampled by those freaky horses?' Umari muttered, his voice shaking.

'Forget that,' Sani said, trying to push away the dark thoughts. 'We need to find him.' But as he spoke, a cold, ghostly sensation crawled over him – like someone's fingers, long and bony, had just run through his hair.

'Who's there?' Sani snapped, spinning around, his heart pounding. But there was no one in sight.

'Come out, you bald-head!' Ray yelled, his voice shaking.

'Y-yeah, c-come out!' Umari said, trying to sound braver than he felt.

A soft breeze curled around them, icy and unsettling, making them shiver. Then, just as they thought they were alone, a low, rasping whisper slithered through the air.

'Do you want your brother back?' the voice murmured, sweet but sinister, carrying a sense of something deeply wrong.

'You better give him back!' Sani shouted, his fists tightening, though his voice trembled, betraying the fear he couldn't control.

The voice laughed cruelly. 'If you want him, you'll have to go through the Room of Doom...and play a game...he will be waiting for you there.'

The air grew thick with the smell of something foul, like rotten leaves or damp earth.

'Where is the Room of Doom?!' Sani yelled, desperation creeping into his voice.

But there was no answer – just a heavy silence that pressed in on them. And then the awful, suffocating feeling that something was watching them.

'This is just great!' Ray yelled, stomping on the floor so hard it sounded like he was trying to start an earthquake. 'I knew we should have stayed back! If I get my hands on this bald-head ghost, I'll squish his face like a pancake, then slap him up! And then, I'll stomp on his twinkle toes like I'm in a tap-dancing contest!'

'Ha! Well, I'll trap him in a jar and shake him like a soda can!' Umari said, puffing out his chest. 'Then I'll let him loose on my pet hamster and watch them battle each other! Who do you think would win, huh? The ghost or Mr. Nibbles the Destroyer?'

Sani rolled his eyes so hard they almost fell out. 'Yeah, real clever, Umari. Well, I'll turn him into a giant slime ball and throw him down the stairs like I'm playing bowling with a wet noodle!'

Ray snorted loudly. 'I'll just throw him into the biggest puddle I can find and let him marinate in the mud like he's a ghost soup! Ghost stew, anyone?'

'That's dumb!' Umari snapped. 'What if he doesn't even *like* mud? What if he's allergic to it like some people are allergic to cats? You ever think about that?'

'Who cares?' Ray grinned. 'It's a ghost! He can't complain. Plus, it's a *perfect* ghost bath!'

Sani placed his hands on his hips, attempting to appear serious, but his face flushed, betraying his struggle to hold back a laugh. 'Stop it, both of you!' he shouted, throwing his hands up in the air like he was trying to catch an invisible basketball. 'We're not going to win by acting like a bunch of idiots! We need a *real* plan, not just...I don't know... putting him in jars or making him do mud facials!'

Ray looked at Sani for a moment, then sighed dramatically. 'Fine. No ghost facials. But I still think the hamster idea was solid.'

'Where do you think this 'Room of Doom' is?' Umari asked, his voice trembling as he glanced around nervously.

'I don't know,' Sani replied, his voice steady despite the tension. 'Let's just start looking.'

He exited the room and led his brothers into the dimly lit hallway.

'I think this ghost is seriously dumb,' Ray muttered, eyeing the red rug sprawled across the floor.

They followed his gaze, their hearts pounding in their chests as the realisation hit them.

'Wet footprints!' Umari shouted, his excitement cutting through his fear. 'They have to be Abner's! If we follow them, they'll lead us straight to him!' A grin spread across his face.

'Yeah, and then we'll see what this 'Room of Doom' is all about,' Ray added, stepping towards the footprints.

'Wait, hold on,' Umari stammered, his voice shaking. 'The 'Room of Doom' – I almost forgot about that,' he muttered, hesitating briefly before reluctantly joining Ray and Sani.

Chapter Five

The air in the hallway grew colder with each step they took, a strange, suffocating chill that clung to their skin like icy fingers.

'Did you hear that?' Sani unexpectedly whispered, his voice barely audible.

Stopping abruptly, Ray squinted into the inky blackness. A faint scratching sound cut through the hallway like sharp claws raking against aged wood. Ray glanced around, but the shadows revealed nothing.

'I didn't hear anything,' Umari said, trying to sound braver than he felt. 'Let's keep moving.'

Sani and Ray didn't need convincing. Abner's wet footprints beckoned them forward, leading them deeper into the house. Each step felt heavier than the last, the walls closing in on them.

They stopped at the bottom of the grand stairs, shivers running like cold needles along their spines. An impossibly long, dark shadow stretched across the first step, untouched by any visible light.

'Upstairs,' Sani croaked, his voice quaking. 'We have to find Abner. Now.'

The trail of wet footprints lured them up the staircase. Ray stepped forward, the stairs groaning beneath his weight as though the house was warning them to stop. Behind him, Sani and Umari hesitated, exchanging uneasy glances before following.

The moment they reached the second floor, everything changed. The silence was unnatural, thick and oppressive. The temperature plummeted, and an unsettling mist began to coil through the air, wrapping around them like unseen hands.

'Did you see that?' Umari whispered, his finger pointing towards the end of the hallway. It looked like a flower floating in the air. Before anyone could answer, the floorboards groaned beneath their feet, and a door slammed shut violently.

Ray, Sani, and Umari stood motionless, their gazes locking onto the door.

'I'm scared,' Umari said softly, his voice barely a whisper. His arms trembled as he hugged himself tightly.

'Don't be silly,' Sani said confidently, offering Umari a reassuring glance. 'We're the Fearsome Four. Nothing can stop us.' He narrowed his eyes, his determination clear as he took a bold step forward.

They made their way down the shadowy hallway, the darkness pressing around them until they reached the end. The trail of footprints stopped abruptly in front of a wooden door, towering over them like a giant watching their every move. The door looked old, its surface scratched and worn as if it had seen many years of secrets.

'You think this is the Room of Doom?' Ray asked, raising an eyebrow and glancing at Sani.

'There's only one way to find out,' Sani said, his voice steady as he grabbed the cold, rusted doorknob. With a grunt, he shoved the door open, and it groaned loudly like an angry beast waking up from a long sleep.

The door groaned open, revealing a vast, empty room cloaked in dull grey. The air inside was stale, heavy with the scent of neglect, as if untouched for years. Ray smirked, his lips curling into a grin. 'Is this it? It doesn't look so doom-y.'

'Abner!' Umari called out, his voice filled with panic as he stepped forward. But before he could walk any further, a blinding white flame shot up from the ground, racing towards the ceiling. It was so hot that Umari could feel the heat on his face; he froze in terror. Just as the flame threatened to touch him, Sani grabbed his arm and yanked him back, pulling him out of danger.

'This room isn't just any room,' Sani muttered, his eyes narrowing in suspicion.

'Guys!' Abner's voice rang out, loud and relieved, cutting through the silence. 'Get me out of here!' The desperation in his tone was unmistakable as they turned to see him trapped inside a cage of thick metal bars at the far end of the room. He looked like a giant bird trapped in a tiny cage, his eyes wide with fear.

'We're coming, just hang on!' Sani called out reassuringly.

Suddenly, the floor beneath their feet rumbled, and without warning, the tiles shot up like jagged teeth, shooting upwards as though designed to strike them. Sani acted instinctively, hauling Umari out of harm's way.

'Move, move, move!' Ray shouted, his voice frantic as they darted around the rising tiles, narrowly avoiding them with every step.

'Just a little further!' Sani urged, his eyes locked on the cage where Abner stood, trapped and helpless.

But then, dark shadows emerged from the room's corners, their movements too quick to follow. The shadows were alive, wrapping around their legs, trying to drag them down.

'H-HELP!' Umari cried, struggling to break free as the shadows tightened their grip around his legs. He kicked and squirmed, but the darkness clung to him like vines.

'Sani!' Ray yelled, reaching out to help Umari. 'The shadows, they're pulling Umari into the ground!'

'Hold on!' Sani shouted, turning towards a nearby rusted iron rod resting on the floor. He broke the dark tendrils holding Umari with a mighty swing, and the shadows hissed, fading away with a ghostly, haunting whisper.

Chapter Six

As they rushed towards the cage, they heard a terrifying roar echoing endlessly through the room. Flames burst forth from behind, hurtling towards them like an unstoppable wave of fire.

'Run!' Sani screamed, his heart racing as they reached the cage.

Abner was shaking with fright, his eyes wide with terror. 'Hurry! Get me out.'

Sani gripped the bars of the cage tightly and yanked with all his strength, but they remained firmly in place. The fire surged forward relentlessly, its heat suffocating and unbearable.

'Come on, come on!' Ray yelled, slamming his shoulder against the bars. The fire was only a few feet away; they had to act fast.

'Umari!' Sani yelled urgently. 'The latch! It's on the side!'

Umari scrambled towards the side of the cage, his heart pounding. He grabbed the latch and yelled, 'How do I open this thing?!' Sweat trickled down his face as he examined the lock. Suddenly, an idea flashed in his mind. Without wasting a moment, he reached into his pocket and pulled out a long K'NEX piece. He jammed it into the latch, twisting and manoeuvring it with precision. 'C'mon, c'mon,' he muttered, gritting his teeth, his eyes darting nervously towards the roaring flames creeping closer.

The lock gave way with a satisfying click, sending the cage door swinging wide open. Abner shot out like a cannonball and wrapped his arms around Umari, hugging him tightly, but Sani quickly grabbed both of them by their arms and yanked them backwards, pulling them away from the dangerous flames.

'No time for hugs!' Sani shouted. 'We need to get out of here, NOW!'

But it was too late – the flames had surrounded them, closing in from all sides.

'We're gonna diiiiiiiiiiiie!' Umari screamed.

'I'm going to miss tonight's pizza!' Ray cried, tears streaming down his face. 'And I'll really miss my sock collection and my favourite chair! I'll never get to finish my game of Lego Men! I didn't even get to eat that last cookie! I didn't say goodbye to my plants! I'll never play my video games again. I didn't even win the final level of *Super Mega Space Fighters*!'

Ray sniffled, wiping away a tear. 'I didn't get to pat my kitten, Mr Grey, one last time, and I never told Mum I loved her...or that I accidentally coloured on her favourite black heels last week. And I didn't get to finish that comic book! It was *just* getting to the good part, a-a-and...!'

Ray's wailing began to sound hideous as he rambled on, 'And I never got to finish my chocolate milk! I was really looking forward to that...AGHHHH!'

With a loud, unsettling sound, the wooden floorboards began to splinter.

'Wha...' Umari managed to utter before the ground collapsed entirely, hurling them downwards in a tangle of limbs.

'OH MY GOSH, WE'RE FALLING!' Abner screamed, his words drowned out by the sharp cracks of breaking wood and the whooshing wind around them.

They plummeted downwards, the world spinning like a crazy carnival ride. They slammed into walls, tumbled into each other, and got covered in dust and debris. It felt like the whole house was crumbling apart.

Ray screamed, 'I never told the pizza guy how much I loved his garlic bread...why didn't I tell him?!!'

'Ray, focus!' Umari shouted, trying to grab onto something as they continued to plummet. But it was no use.

With a final thundering crash, they landed in a jumbled heap on the floor, groaning and gasping for breath.

'Are we dead?' Ray muttered, his face a mixture of horror and confusion. 'Because if we are, then I never even got to eat my chocolate stash under the bed!'

Umari swung his fist and struck Ray hard across the head. 'Shut up, big baby!' he snapped, his spit splattering across Ray's face.

'Why do you always do that?!' Ray yelled, wiping spit off his cheek. Then he paused dramatically. 'Wait, I'm not dead!' He sprang to his feet and performed a silly, joyful dance, wiggling his bottom. 'Ouch, my head and my backside really hurt!'

'Nooo! How did you pesky little brats survive?' a sudden voice rasped from the shadows.

The boys' eyes widened in terror as the ghostly figure they had seen on the cobbled path materialised before them. Its pale, glowing skin contrasted sharply against the darkness, and its red eyes gleamed like burning embers.

The ghost lounged lazily on a black, throne-like chair, watching them with a sinister gaze.

'We survived 'cause we're the Fearsome Four!' Sani yelled, stepping forward, his voice trembling but defiant.

The ghost tilted its head, its lips curling into an evil grin. 'Oh, how cute,' it sneered. 'A bunch of little bogey boys who think they're fearless. But you're just rats in the dark, scurrying to survive.' With a flick of its hand, it hurled something upwards and seized it midair with its bony fingers.

Chapter Seven

'You dare call me and my brothers bogey boys, you fool!' Umari shouted, his voice shaking with fury as spit flew from his mouth again. 'You'll regret it!'

Abner, his face flushed with anger, glared at the ghost. 'And stop playing with my glasses like they're a toy!' he snapped.

The ghost's laugh was cold and bone-chilling as it slowly floated off the black throne, its red eyes glowing brighter. 'Get out of my house before I turn you into stone,' it hissed, 'and you won't be getting your precious glasses back.' The ghost glided towards them and shouted. 'Leave! NOW!'

Abner held his ground, arms crossed, his gaze locked onto the ghost. 'Not until you give my glasses back,' he said with determination, his eyes narrowing.

The ghost made a loud clicking sound with its bony fingers, and a glowing white circle materialised in the corner of the room. The circle expanded, growing larger and larger until it formed into an ugly ape-like figure, its skin pale and stretched tight over its bones. The creature's eyes were hollow, its mouth dripping with something foul.

The ghost threw the glasses across the room, sending them sliding and clattering loudly on the cold, hard floor.

The ape's enormous hand shot out in the blink of an eye, swiftly snatching them up.

With a terrifying growl, it shoved the glasses into its mouth and swallowed them whole.

'Sorry about that,' the ghost taunted, its red eyes shining as it watched the boys' terrified faces. 'Ghost Ape! Stomp on these wretched kids and crumble them,' it rasped, its voice dripping with malice.

'Oh no,' Umari gasped, his voice shaky. 'We're gonna be squashed like playdough under that ape's huge hands and feet!'

'RUN!' Ray screamed, his voice filled with panic. Without thinking, he dashed towards the nearby door, pulling the handle, but it wouldn't budge. 'It's locked!' he shrieked, his eyes wild with fear as he turned towards his brothers.

The ape lumbered towards them, its massive feet thudding against the floor with each step, shaking the ground beneath them. The boys' teeth clattered uncontrollably.

'Stomp! Stomp!' the ape growled, its footsteps shaking the house to its core. Its eyes were fixed on the boys. The walls creaked and groaned, and the house quaked with every movement.

Suddenly, out of nowhere, the booming strike of hooves against the floor filled the room, resonating like rolling thunder. The boys watched in horror as fifteen horses appeared out of nowhere, galloping around the room.

'I'm gonna become a mashed potato,' Umari sobbed, his voice trembling as he stared at the ape before him.

'Stomp! Stomp!' the ape continued to growl, raising its huge hands. Umari squeezed his eyes shut, bracing for the crushing blow, his heart pounding as he prepared to be flattened like playdough.

'Back off, monkey face!' Sani shouted, swinging a rusty metal pole with all his strength. It smashed into the ape's thick leg with a loud thud, the sound cutting through the chaos.

The ape froze, its eyes widening with fury. 'Me no monkey face! ME APE FACE!' it roared, its voice shaking the walls, making Sani spin around in panic and flee. The ape charged towards Sani at terrifying speed.

The horses galloped around them, their hooves hitting the ground forcefully, making everything feel dizzy and out of control.

'Grab that metal pole!' Abner called out to Ray, his voice barely audible over the chaos.

Ray darted towards a pole lying on the floor, sweat trickling down his forehead. He grabbed it, then turned his gaze towards Abner.

'What do I do with it?' he shouted, his voice lost in the thunder of hooves, the ape's roars, and Sani's frantic shouts.

'Beat that monkey face!' Abner shouted, grabbing another rusty pole from the floor. Without any further hesitation, he charged at the ape, his legs pumping like pistons.

Sani was seconds away from being crushed when Abner and Ray's poles slammed into the ape's powerful legs. *Thwack! Thwack!* The sound reverberated through the room as they struck the ape with all their strength.

'Take that! Monkey face!' Ray yelled, performing a spinning martial arts move and hitting the ape's foot with his pole.

The ape grabbed Ray and flung him like a tennis ball across the room.

'Aaaaaagh!' Ray shrieked. 'Noooo! I can't fly!' he wailed as he soared through the air, only to crash straight into a massive window. The curtains flew apart, letting sunlight pour into the room. Ray slid down the glass like a squashed bug and landed on the floor with a thud.

'Phew!' he laughed, 'I survived!'

The ape let out a deep, guttural roar, but then...something bizarre happened. The sunlight filtering through the window and stretching across the floor touched its massive foot. The creature recoiled, hopping backwards as if it had stepped on a sharp piece of Lego.

Sani observed the scene, his eyes narrowing. Then he gasped. 'The ape doesn't like light! Look, its ghostly body is starting to vanish!'

As he continued to whack the ape's legs with all his might, Abner yelled, 'So sunlight is the ape's worst nightmare? Perfect! Let's bring in more light!'

'Yeah! Umari, open all the curtains in this room!' Sani shouted, swinging his metal pole at the ape's arm. 'We'll distract him. Go!'

Umari froze briefly, staring at the fifteen massive windows around the room. Then, with a deep breath, he darted towards the nearest one and yanked the curtains open. Sunlight streamed in, cutting through the darkness.

A raspy, chilling voice screeched, 'NO! NO! Shut those curtains!'

Umari spun around to see the ghost materialise from the shadows, its glowing red eyes fixed on him. The ghost floated closer, bony hands reaching out. 'Close them NOW!' it hissed.

But Umari didn't flinch. He sprinted towards the next curtain and yanked it open. The ghost let out a horrible wail, trying to drift towards the window and shut the curtains, but the sunlight drove it back. Its form shimmered and twisted as it hid behind the massive black throne.

'Stop it!' the ghost hissed. 'Shut those curtains! I can't live in this house if it's filled with light!' Its crimson eyes burned with rage, but its trembling figure betrayed its fear.

Chapter Eight

'Take that! And that!' roared Abner, repeatedly slamming the pole into the ape's stomach. The creature staggered and began to choke. Its massive hands clutched its throat, and then - *PLOP!* - something flew out of its mouth.

'My glasses!' Abner yelled, a radiant smile spreading across his face. He dropped the pole and darted forward. 'Yahoo!' he cheered, scooping them off the floor. One of the lenses was cracked, but he didn't care. With a grin, he slid them onto his face.

'Perfect! Now, what was I doing...' Abner began, but his words faded as the ape grabbed him by the hair, lifting him off the floor with ease. Abner flapped his arms like a wild duck as the beast brought him towards its huge, drooling mouth.

'Uh, guys?' Abner squeaked. 'Little help here?'

Sani gasped in horror as he watched his big brother dangle helplessly in the air, ready to become the ape's snack.

'Nooooooooo!' shrieked the ghost from behind the throne. It cowered deeper into the shadows. 'I hate light! I *hate* light!' it hissed, its raspy voice trembling with fury and fear.

Umari was about to open the last curtain when the ghost suddenly shot towards him, its icy fingers clamping down on his arm. 'Close all these curtains, you little wretch,' it hissed, its voice dripping with venom.

'Get off me!' Umari stammered, his breath hitching as he struggled to break free.

'Let him go!' Ray shouted, his voice filled with fury. 'Or I'll open the last curtain, I swear!' Without waiting for the ghost to answer, he yanked the curtain open in a swift, forceful motion, letting in a flood of blinding light.

The thunderous rhythm of the horses' hooves gradually diminished, their echoes fading into the distance as their towering, shadowy forms began to blur with each passing second. An uncanny stillness settled over the room, the last faint reverberations of their galloping now gone.

One by one, the spectral horses dissolved into the air, their figures dissipating like wisps of mist, leaving behind an unsettling stillness.

Meanwhile, the giant ape held Abner high above its wide-open mouth, ready to swallow him whole. With a horrible grunt, it opened its mouth even wider, the dark pit inside looking like a deadly trap. But just before it could close its mouth and swallow Abner, the light streaming from the windows washed over the ape.

The light poured over it like a flood, and the ape began to fade, its massive frame quivering. With a painful roar, the ape's body started to crumble apart, and within moments, it was gone. Its terrifying form dissolved into thin air, leaving only a faint glow that quickly vanished.

Abner plummeted to the floor like a sack of potatoes, the impact so loud it seemed to rattle the entire house. 'Ouch, my butt!' he groaned, rubbing the point of impact.

The ghost gripping Umari's arm let out an ear-piercing shriek. 'I despise the light!' it wailed, its translucent face twisting in agony. Suddenly, a brilliant surge of light pierced through the room, radiating brighter than the combined glow of a hundred suns. The ghost's scream turned into a distorted howl as its shadowy form began to dissolve. Within seconds, it vanished, leaving only a haunting echo of its final, sorrowful cry.

Umari rubbed his arm where the ghost had grabbed him and then shook his head. 'Is this real?' he whispered, his eyes wide. Then he suddenly boomed, 'Did we just kick some ghost butt?!'

'Uhhh…' Ray paused dramatically, scratching his chin. 'I don't think you'd wanna have your trainer connecting with a ghost's butt 'cause if you did, your trainer would probably turn greener than your boogers.'

'Hey, my boogers aren't green!' Umari shot back.

'Then what colour are they?' Abner laughed, crossing his arms like he'd just solved a mystery.

'My boogers are unique,' Umari said proudly. 'They're purple. Like royalty.'

'Well, at least I'm not dead, and I can still have pizza tonight,' Ray said, rubbing his flat tummy.

'Yummy!' Sani said, licking his lips like a pizza-loving monster. 'Hey, I heard you've got a secret stash of chocolate hidden under your bed. You gonna share?'

Ray's eyes went as wide as saucers. 'How do you know that?!'

'Cause you howled it out when you thought it was the end of us!' Abner let out a snort, his laughter bubbling uncontrollably.

'Oh, well, I guess I can share,' Ray said, his cheeks turning as red as a tomato.

'Wait, now we know who coloured on Mum's favourite heels,' Sani said, raising an eyebrow. 'I can't wait to tell her.'

'OOOOPS!' Ray groaned, holding his head like he had just realised he was about to get into trouble.

'You shouldn't be saying 'Oops' to us,' Umari retorted. 'You should be saying it to Mum.'

Ray waved his hands like he was trying to swat away a fly. 'I didn't say 'Oops' because I coloured on the heels! I said, 'Oops,' because I just farted. That'll blow any remaining ghost away!'

The boys all burst into laughter, holding their sides like they'd just heard the funniest joke ever.

Then Sani raised his hand for a high five. 'Fearsome Four!'

And they all roared together, 'FEARSOME FOUR!'

Chapter Nine

'Mum! Dad!' Umari called out, dashing across the meadow towards his parents, who were busy arranging a picnic on the lush, sunlit grass.

'What's all the excitement about, Umari?' Dad asked, placing a carton of orange juice on the picnic mat. 'Are you ready to share one of your famous stories?'

'Yes, Dad! We went into this creepy, old house and got rid of a nasty ghost,' Umari exclaimed, his eyes wide with excitement.

'Oh, really? That sounds...spooky!' Mum said with a playful grin, pretending to believe him.

'Then out came this massive, bald-headed ape!' Ray shouted, throwing himself into a frenzied stomp. His exaggerated moves had everyone roaring with laughter.

'That's quite an adventure,' Dad chuckled. 'I love how creative you kids are.'

'Dad, we're *not* making it up!' Sani groaned, throwing his hands into the air. 'It was real! We almost got trampled by horses as well!'

'Yeah! There were *lots* of them!' Umari added, stretching his arms out as wide as they could go.

Dad smiled. 'When I was your age, I used to make up wild stories like this,' he said, grinning as he handed out sandwiches to the boys.

Ray paused mid-bite. 'Didn't you think it was weird that it rained and thundered in the middle of summer?' he asked.

Mum frowned, lowering her cup of orange juice. 'It didn't rain, and it definitely didn't thunder,' she said firmly.

The boys exchanged uneasy glances and began eating slowly.

Abner groaned loudly. 'Mum, I broke my glasses. I'm really sorry,' he said, removing them and handing them over.

Mum inspected them with a small smile. 'Don't try to trick me. These aren't broken,' she said, passing them back.

Abner's jaw dropped. 'Wait, what? The ape destroyed the lens, yet somehow, it's not broken!' he gasped. 'We couldn't have imagined everything, the ghosts, the rickety house. It was *real*!'

Dad laughed, shaking his head. 'You boys and your wild imaginations.'

After finishing their snacks, the boys dashed off, racing down the meadow.

'This is so weird,' Sani muttered. 'It wasn't just imagination. Zombies and ghosts, they're real. I know it.'

'Yeah,' Umari agreed with a long sigh.

Ray's foot hit a worn, rusted manhole cover, making him trip. His hands hit the ground hard, the impact leaving a sharp sting that quickly turned to a dull ache.

'Ow...' he muttered, shaking his stinging palms and glaring at the manhole cover.

'Are you okay?' Umari gasped, his eyes darting towards Ray's reddened hands.

'Kinda...' Ray said, standing up and dusting himself off.

RIBBIT! RIBBIT!

'What was that?' Sani's voice trembled slightly as he raised an eyebrow.

'It sounded like...a toad. A huge one,' Abner whispered, his face pale.

'A-a-a huge toad?' Umari stammered, instinctively stepping closer to the group.

'It sounded like it came from...down there.' Ray pointed to the manhole cover. His voice dropped to a whisper. 'Maybe it's under there.'

Sani crouched beside the manhole. 'Let's check it out,' he said, his curiosity battling with his fear.

'You're kidding, right?' Umari whispered, his voice trembling.

But Ray was already kneeling next to Sani, his hands gripping the edge of the cover. 'Help me lift it.'

Abner and Umari hesitated momentarily before stepping forward to help lift the cover. Their fingers dug into its rough, cold edges, their breaths trembling with uncertainty. With a united heave, they lifted it.

'AAAAAAAAAAAAGH!' they all screamed together.

A glowing yellow eye bulged out of the manhole, slick and covered in sticky, slimy goo. It was huge, far bigger than any eye should be. The eye didn't blink; it just stared at them like it was waiting for something. The air around them felt thick and foul like something had been left to rot for too long. The ground seemed to shake beneath their feet, and then, with a slow, gross squelch, the eye blinked once, making their skin crawl.

Without thinking, Abner grabbed the manhole cover and, with all his strength, slammed it down onto the eye.

SLAM!

The filthy sound of squelching goo echoed around them as if the cover had crushed something wet and horrible beneath it.

Sani, wide-eyed and pale, let out a shaky breath and gulped. 'I think we're in for another Fearsome Four adventure!'

Upcoming Titles By Joseph Jethro:

- Fearsome Four: The Toad of the Grimy Underworld
- Fearsome Four: The Witch of Nightwood School
- Fearsome Four: Stenchfang the King of Poo
- Fearsome Four: The Beast of the Rocky Mountains
- Fearsome Four: The Butcher Next Door
- Fearsome Four: The Appliances of the Kitchen Downstairs
- Fearsome Four: The Captain of the Snot Monsters
- Fearsome Four: Terror Baby of the Giants